A Day
at the
Beach

by Geoff Patton
illustrated by David Clarke

RISING STARS

to the beach

to Sam's house

to Emily's house

the supermarket

Con's house

2

to the
museum

Lin's
apartment

3

Hi. My name is Con.
This is my family. Do you know
where we are going today?

Chapter 1
Packing the Car

We are going to the beach. I help Dad pack the car. I pack my bat and ball. I pack my sunhat and sun shirt. I pack my Superhero Space Tent.

Dad says, 'Con, we are only going to the beach for one day. You don't need your Superhero Space Tent.'

I say to Dad, 'What if it rains and we all get wet?' I say, 'What if the sun gets too hot and we all melt?' But Dad says, 'No way, Con.'

Sometimes Dad is no fun.

Chapter 2
Squashed in the Car

On the way to the beach I sit next to my big brother Tom. Tom is too big. I say to Mum, 'Tom is squashing me.'

Tom is squashing me.

I say, 'Tom is mashing me.' I say, 'If Tom doesn't stop squashing and mashing me, I will be like a jellyfish by the time we get to the beach.'

I say to Mum, 'Can I sit in the front seat?'
But Mum says, 'No way, Con.'

10

Sometimes Mum is no fun.

Chapter 3
A Very Big Sandcastle

At the beach I make a sandcastle.
I make a big sandcastle. I want to
make the biggest sandcastle in the
world, but my sister Maria is in
the way.

I say, 'Maria, I am making a big
sandcastle.' I say, 'If you move
I can make a bigger sandcastle.'

I say to Maria, 'If you move I can make the biggest sandcastle in the world.'
But my sister says, 'No way, Con.'

Sometimes my sister is no fun.

Chapter 4
Ball at the Beach

At the beach Tom plays with my bat and ball. I say, 'Can I play too?' Tom says, 'Con, this game is for big kids.'

I say, 'I am big.' I say, 'If you don't let me play, I hope that you hit the ball in the water. I hope it is eaten by a fish and the fish is eaten by a shark.'

I say to Tom, 'Please can I play?'
But my brother says, 'No way, Con.'

Sometimes my brother is no fun.

Chapter 5
Superhero Space Tent

At the beach I see my friend Sam.
He is playing in his Superhero
Space Tent.

Sam says, 'Do you want to play in my
Superhero Space Tent?'
I say, 'Yes.'
I say, 'I think it is going to rain.'
It starts to rain.

Dad says, 'Hey Con, can I come in?'
Mum says, 'Hey Con, can I come in?'
Tom says, 'Hey Con, can I come in?'
Maria says, 'Hey Con, can I come in?'

I say, 'No way, Dad. No way, Mum.'
I say, 'No way, Tom. No way, Maria.'

Survival Tips

1 Always pack your own bag. That way you can sneak in more stuff.

2 Get to the car first so you can get a window seat.

3 Leave your brother and sister at home.

22

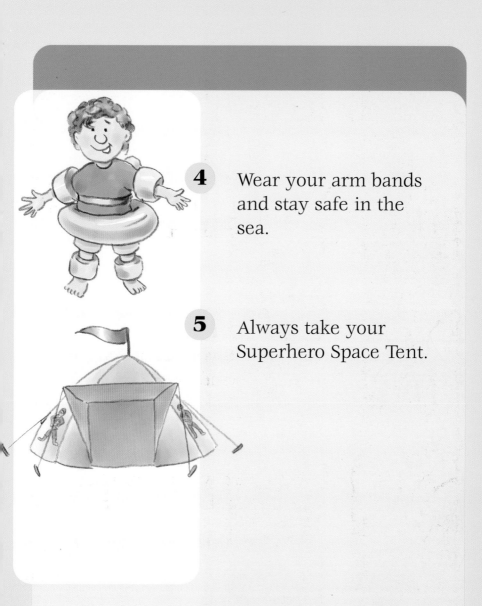

4 Wear your arm bands and stay safe in the sea.

5 Always take your Superhero Space Tent.

Riddles and Jokes

Sam	How do baby fish swim?
Con	They do the crawl.

Con	Why did the teacher wear sunglasses to the beach?
Sam	Because her pupils were so bright.

Con	How do you talk to a fish under water?
Sam	Drop it a line.

Sam	What did the sea say to the sand?
Con	Nothing. It just waved.

Con	Why did Tom and Maria get out of the water?
Sam	Because the sea weed.